Crusty Cupcake Presents: The Christmas Weed

Sarviol Publishing

ISBN: 9781792131820

Special wholesale and re-sale rates are available. For more information,
please contact Deb Harvest at petethepopcorn@gmail.com

When purchasing this book, please consider purchasing
an additional copy to donate to your local library.

Written by: Nick Rokicki & Joseph Kelley
Illustrated by: Ronaldo Florendo

Twas' the month of December in Toledo, Ohio. Despite Christmas upcoming, the gloom had set in. Dreary skies, blustery arctic winds and snowflakes fluttering, far and near.

Emrick the Evergreen Cupcake was strolling along, bundled up from the breezes. At the corner of Alexis and Secor, she gazed at a gangly, gray, gawky, overgrown branch...

"Dad, look at that thing. It looks so lonely, leftover from summer," said Emrick. " But it also looks rather grand, still standing tall after the fall."

"Grand? That Weed looks grand?" said the Dad.

"There's only one thing that could make that Weed look grander!" exclaimed Emrick, suddenly feeling a rush of Holiday cheer. "Some garland and glitz and glitter goes great at this glorious time of year."

Reaching into her shopping bag, Emrick the Evergreen Cupcake began prodding and pulling, poking and perusing until she tastefully trotted out the tinsel she was looking for. Wrapping the decoration ever-so-carefully around the tattered old tree, it slowly took on a new life.

"Well, Emrick... I calculate that you are correct. The Toledo Christmas Weed is grand... in a Toledo type of way," said her Father.

"Dad! Stop calling it a Weed!" complained Emrick, as the two continued on their walk, leaving footprints in the fresh-fallen snow.

The very next morning, Emrick the Evergreen Cupcake was skipping along to school when she saw the cast of cupcakes congregated at Alexis and Secor.

Tate the Tannenbaum Cupcake was thoughtfully settling a skirt around the base of the branch.

Secor

Sandy the Shining Star Cupcake
was straddled on the shoulders of
Shawna the Snow Cupcake,
scrupulously sticking a small star
at the summit of the shoot.

Christopher the Christmas Cookie
Cupcake tied a trio of trimmings
in red, white and blue.

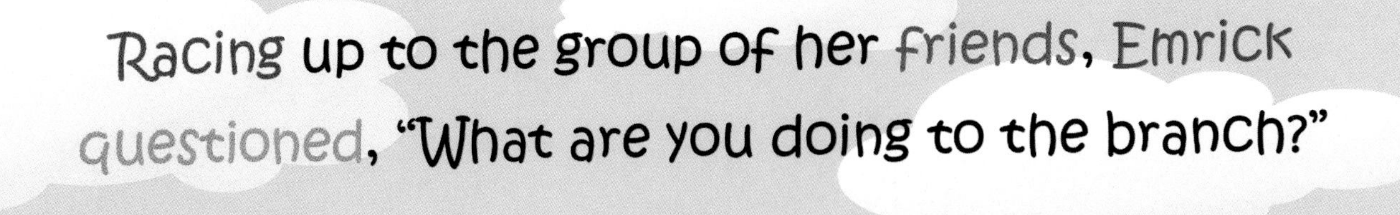

Racing up to the group of her friends, Emrick questioned, "What are you doing to the branch?"

"The branch? It's a Weed! And we wanted to add our part!" explained Shawna.

"Ugh! Why does everyone keep calling it a Weed?!?! That makes it sound so ugly," said Emrick.

"Whatever you want to call it, you can't deny that it is kind of ugly ... but that Weed also makes me feel really happy," added Tate, hassling his friends to hurry along. "We're gonna be late to school!"

The school day dragged, as those leading up to vacation tend to do. Emrick envisioned the branch breaking down due to the density of the decorations. Tate thought of twisting ties of turquoise twine to the tree. Sandy and Shawna schemed to sprinkle shimmery sparkles of snowflakes. But none of their imaginations could prepare them for the reality that they'd see while wandering home from school.

"Hey! You can't cut down the Weed!"
said Emrick, running up to Gabriel the
Garland Cupcake, holding garden
cutters in his hands.

"We decorated that Weed for all the Cupcakes to see!" said Christopher the Christmas Cookie Cupcake.
"I'm under direct orders from Mayor Marty the Merry Cupcake to cut down this Weed," said Gabriel. "Step aside."

The friends were lost at what to do... so they did the first thing that came to their cupcake heads. Holding hands, Emrick, Tate, Sandy, Shawna and Christopher formed a circle around the Weed and started singing, "Oh Christmas Weed, Oh Christmas Weed, Oh how you look so pretty..."

Throwing his hands high above his head in exasperation, not wanting to cause a scene with these Cupcake Kiddos, Gabriel the Garland Cupcake retreated to his Jeep, grabbing his phone. “Hello, Mayor Marty? These kids won’t let me cut down the Weed!”

"Mr. Garland... tear down that Weed! It's an eyesore to this City and it won't be tolerated," declared Mayor Marty the Merry Cupcake... who obviously wasn't feeling too merry.

"But, Mr. Mayor... it's actually, well... it makes me kind of peaceful," said the Garland Cupcake.

"The Weed... it makes you peaceful?" pondered the Mayor. "This, I have to see for myself."

That evening, hidden under wintertime
darkness, Mayor Marty the Merry Cupcake
and Gabriel the Garland Cupcake made
their move. Creeping across the corner of
Alexis and Secor, they saw the Weed.

Just as Gabriel removed his garden cutters, Crusty the Carrot Cupcake stepped out from behind the lamppost.

"Calm, calm," came the voice of Crusty, motioning to the street corners nearby. "Can't you see what this Weed is doing for the Christmas Spirit?" Indeed, boxes had been placed nearby, labeled: Chow for Cupcakes in Craving, Christmas Charity for Kiddos, along with Coats for Cupcakes.

"The Cupcake Community is coming together in the Christmas Spirit with kindness and giving," said Crusty. "Just let the Weed be, Mr. Mayor!"

"Two days, Crusty! I give it two days until this... Weed... becomes a catastrophe!" said the Mayor, red in the face, rushing away from the scene before he could be seen.

Crusty the Carrot Cupcake knew the Mayor was wrong. He'd seen the sparkle in the eyes of cupcakes both young and old as they came to see the Toledo Christmas Weed.

Troy the Tinsel Cupcake tugged along a tote, towering over with toys of every shape and size. Dumping each one in the box for donations, his mother explained to a nearby news crew that Troy had taken money from his birthday in order to buy gifts to give to less fortunate cupcakes.

Jackson the Jingle Bell Cupcake juggled cans of food at the corner near the Weed, encouraging other cupcakes to drop off food for charities and shelters.

Peyton the Poinsettia Cupcake paraded
around the Weed, passionately praising
Christmas through carols and songs.

Fran the Fruitcake Cupcake came to the tree to share her Famous Flaming Fudge Floatie... kinda like hot chocolate... to warm the Cupcakes who gathered.
14

Gwyneth the Gift Cupcake genuinely lived up to her name, setting up a table where she would wrap gifts for Cupcakes in exchange for donations to charity.
DONATION

Sullivan the Stocking Cupcake gathered coats and capes and cloaks, so that all of the cupcakes in the City had something warm to cover them for the upcoming Winter.

Tegan the Turkey Cupcake, Hailey the Ham Cupcake and Carter the Cranberry Cupcake worked as a team to provide a traditional Holiday meal for homeless cupcakes at a local shelter.

News of The Christmas Weed began spreading throughout the land. The Capitol Crumb newspaper splashed a headline across the front page! Cupcake Tonight ran a television report! Even Stephen Cupbert, the late-night cupcake joined in!

The Capitol Crumb
The Leader in News / visit: www.thecapitolcrumb.com
THE CHRISTMAS WEED
TONIGHT
TONIGHT with
stephen
cupbert

The Weed had grown into a very special place in the heart of the Cupcake Community. For many, the Weed brought happiness. For some, it brought laughter. But for most, it was the renewed sense of the

Christmas Spirit that the Weed gave.

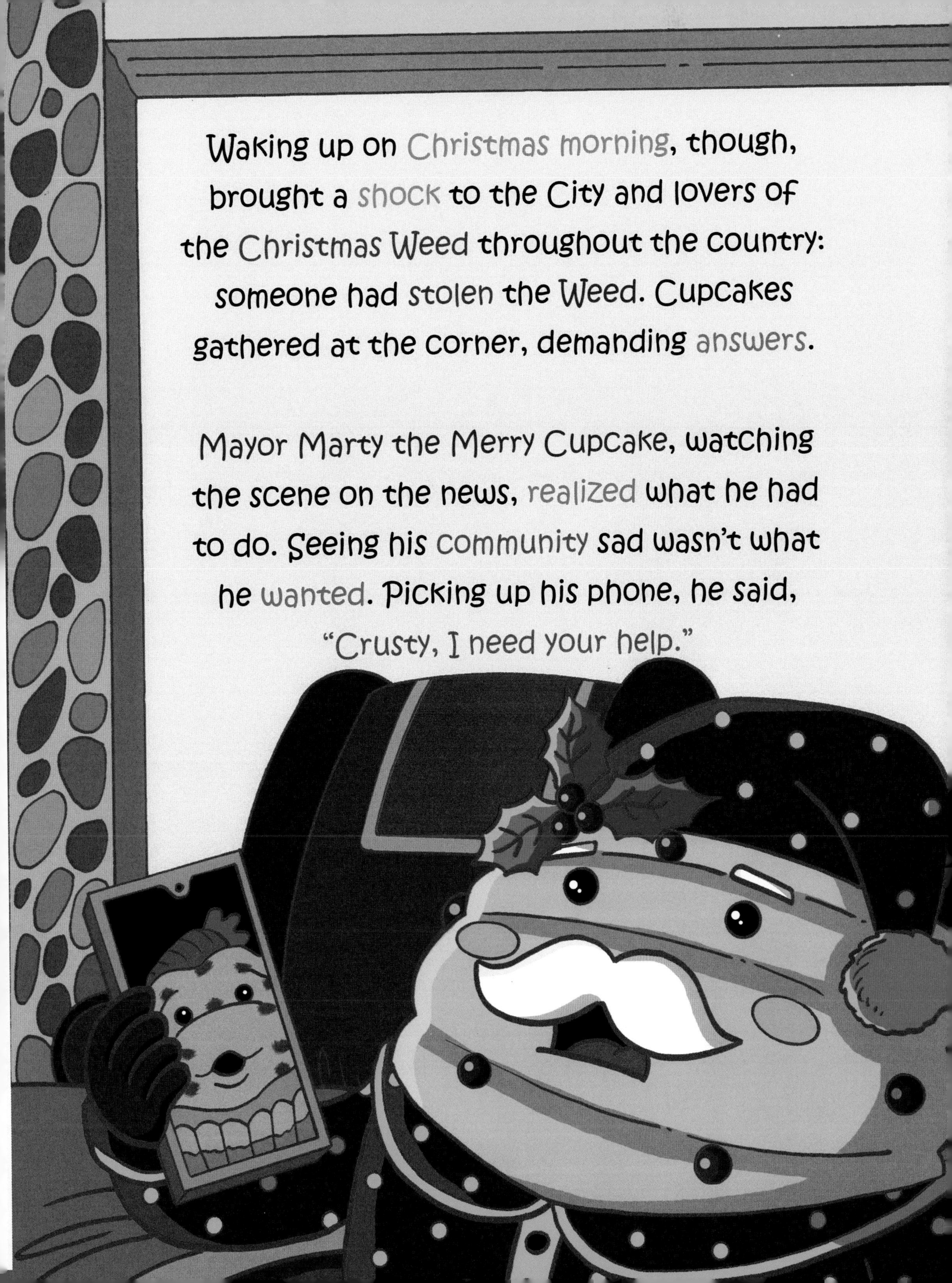

Waking up on Christmas morning, though, brought a shock to the City and lovers of the Christmas Weed throughout the country: someone had stolen the Weed. Cupcakes gathered at the corner, demanding answers.

Mayor Marty the Merry Cupcake, watching the scene on the news, realized what he had to do. Seeing his community sad wasn't what he wanted. Picking up his phone, he said, "Crusty, I need your help."

Together, Crusty and Mayor Marty lifted a tall, dead houseplant from the corner of the Mayor's Office, high above the City.

Cupcakes came out of their homes to help the duo. As they came closer to Alexis and Secor, the crowd began to clear, singing, "Oh Christmas Weed, Oh Christmas Weed..."

Tommy the Twinkle Cupcake began twirling around the Weed, theatrically trimming it with tinsel of every color. Sophia the Sleigh Cupcake did the same, working in tandem. Other cupcakes joined in, making the new Christmas Weed just as spectacular as the first. The Cupcakes knew that it wasn't really the Weed itself that had brought them together, but the mysterious Christmas Spirit that permeates even the grouchiest among us.

Looking from afar,
Emrick the Evergreen Cupcake
peered up at her Dad.
"I guess it was a Weed, after all."

"Well, like your friend Tate said... whatever we call it," responded her Father, "look at all of the Christmas Spirit you helped bring in 2018... and perhaps beyond!"

The creation of this book was funded through pre-sales, which also included a printed dedication in the back of the book. Thank you to these readers and everyone else who participated! -Nick and Joe

Thanks to Ray and Jamie for their support of the book and for showing up at the Christmas Weed!

Dedicated to my granddaughters: Jade, Lilly, Gracie, Ella and Payton. May your hearts always be filled with the joy of giving, loving, sharing and caring... both at Christmas time and the whole year through. Love, Grammie Teena

I dedicate this book to the memory of my parents, Mary and Lawrence Morgan and to the students and teachers of Toledo Public Schools, especially Oakdale Elementary: May the story of the Christmas Weed inspire courageous kindness in our hearts and a persistent desire to always be there for each other. Keep reading! Therese Gordon and Family

Merry Christmas from The Rublaitus Family - Beverly, Stephen (SJJ '89), Mike (SJJ '90), Michelle (NDA '95)

To all those who have supported "The Christmas Weed," may it grow tall and be beautifully decorated for the 2019 Holiday Season and beyond.

Thank you Nick and Joe for bringing the amazing story of kindness, empathy and joy to life. Love Rob, Marc and Keigan.

I was deeply touched by the The Christmas Weed in 2018 and what it meant in our community. It was something so out of the ordinary... how a small weed brought people together, giving them hope and joy, and a spirit of love and giving.
The Christmas Weed of 2018 is my favorite Christmas memory ever. When I went to visit The Christmas Weed, I met people there who drove over 3 hours to see it. Simply unforgettable. If one person can cast a light and light up a community just imagine... All my best wishes, Carol Kiley

Alex Hritz and Kayleigh Salisbury

Judy (Smith) Gill, Christmas 2018

Madisella from Gigi and Pop Pop, Amy Gill, Toledo Ohio

Katie McInerney, always believe in magic and miracles! Love, Mom and Dad, Tammy and Michael McInerney

The Christmas Weed brought people together and gave many hope! So many people worked together to grow a beautiful sense of community. I think reading books is one of the greatest ways for one to grow and learn! As a teacher, reading aloud to my students helps them learn and helps me promote a positive learning community!!
Pat O'Connor

Dedicated to all the friends & family of Wyndy Broome & Patricia Watrol in Toledo, Rossford, Perrysburg & Oregon OH.

To Lexi & Felicity: Thank you for going with me to see the "Christmas Weed." May you always find joy in the little things. - Karru

Merry Christmas from The Kachenmeister's!

The Logan "BRATS" Clan, est. 1995

I dedicate this book to my Great Grandson, Jaxson Brobst and Granddaughter Carlisle Schmidt

Nick and Joe, thank you for embracing an entrepreneurial spirit and writing books that have such an impact on children's lives! Crystal Puckett, Florida

Alexandria and Benjamin Logan, Milton, Ontario, Canada and Isla, Perrey and Beau Johnson, Oakville, Ontario, Canada

Meowy Christmas from Ben, Kendra and Hayden Williams

A sample pencil sketch of Ronaldo Florendo to one of the scenes. http://www.behance.net/rmflorendo14

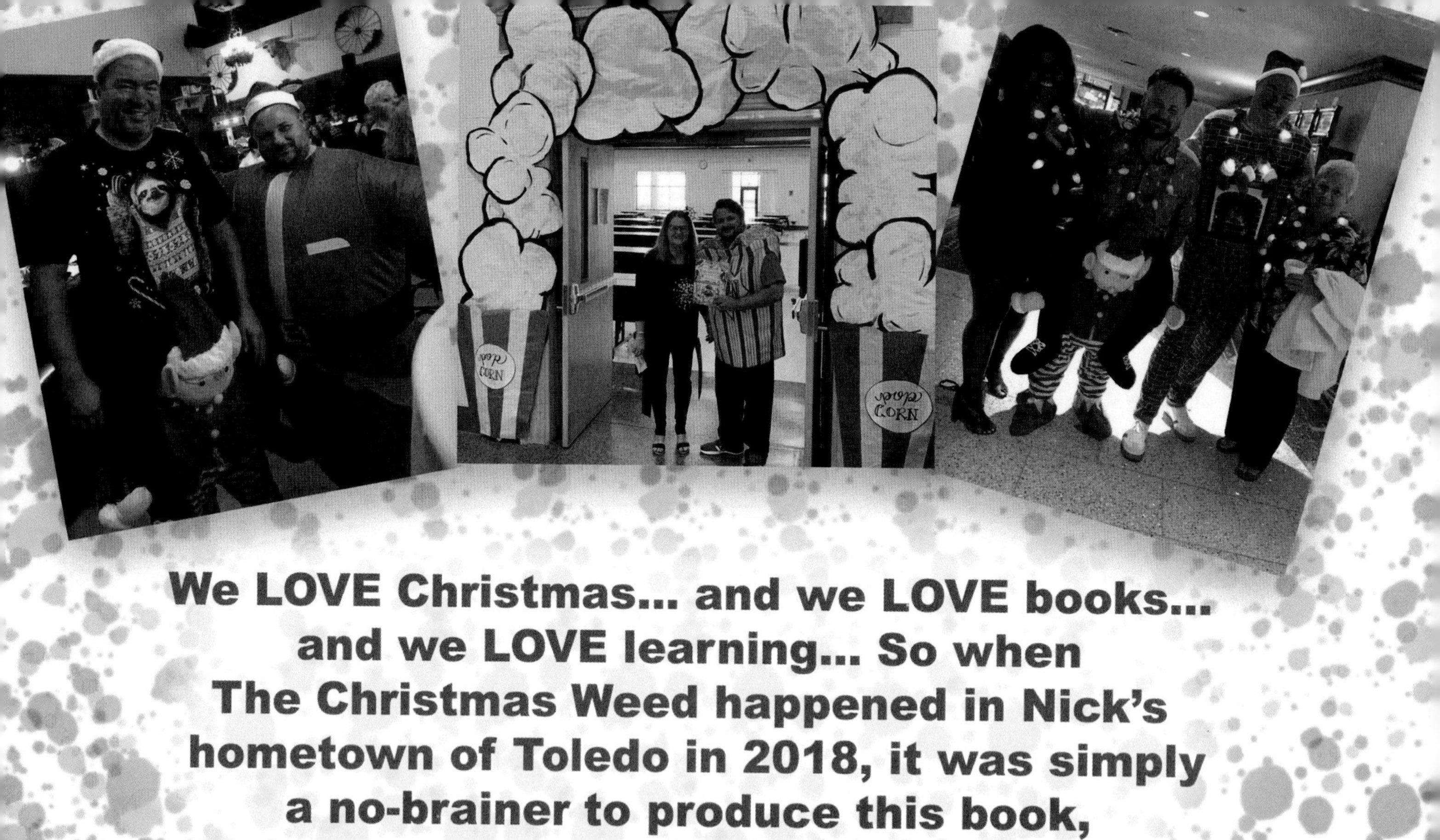

We LOVE Christmas... and we LOVE books... and we LOVE learning... So when The Christmas Weed happened in Nick's hometown of Toledo in 2018, it was simply a no-brainer to produce this book, chock full of great lessons for children. The biggest one? It is SO important to take joy in the simple things during the Christmas season and ALL YEAR through! We know you'll enjoy the story... and complete your collection at petethepopcorn.com!

Merry Christmas!

Nick and Joe

Made in the USA
Monee, IL
03 December 2019

17845323R10031